The Greatest Love Book You'll Ever Read

I0626165

Based on a True Story

By

Manny Ventura

CONTENTS

Chapter 31:

Dedications:

I dedicate this novelette to the creator of all, God for allowing me to ignite my passion in this story. He always finds a way to re-define my purpose in my life. God allows me to challenge my fears and live to my fullest potential, for without Him, I would not have this energetic passion to write this love story.

Also, I would like to dedicate this novelette to my mother and father for guiding me in this thing called life! I do this for them.

Lastly, I dedicate this novelette to everyone who has a love story to tell. We all have our individual paths of love- I hope you enjoy mine.

Most Importantly,
Always Believe in Love
-Manny Ventura

Acknowledgements:

In writing this novelette, I need to thank a few people that made this work come true.

First, I would like to thank my editor Cynthia Alvarez for putting up with my word selections, style of writing, and the crazy love stories I told her about. Cynthia, I really appreciate you for this one! I also want to thank everyone who gave me support and encouragement in my journey into writing this novelette.

Lastly, I wrote this novelette to inspire you to write your story. Everyone has a story to tell. If you ever had passion to create something in life go after that dream and never give up.

Most Importantly,
Always Believe in Love
-Manny Ventura

Please don't... those were the last words I remember. Her smile wasn't the same. Her happiness was gone...

Chapter *1:*

The Girl in The Corner of the Room

Ever since I saw her for the first time I knew I was in love. Ninth grade. 2006. Ms. George's class and a smoking hot girl sat in the corner of the room. I was the real cool type right, I played on the football team, had strong buff arms and was cool as water. I peeked over nonchalantly to take a full glance and I couldn't believe it... I was in love. She had this stunning look that let you know she was special. One time, she wore this beautiful red flowery dress with round earrings that complimented her caramel complexion. Her eyes were sudden and bold and grasped an emotional indepthness that drew you in closely, making sure you never let go. She was the one girl that held my heart and guided with me passion. I was only fifteen years old at the time and I never knew what love felt like, but I hoped one day I would marry a queen and I be her King. I loved her to the moon and back and I would go on to do anything just to be next to her. She was my heart, my beloved sunshine, and best of all she was the reason my heart still smiles. But of course, the story didn't start off that way.

1

Chapter 2:

I'm Sprung

Those eyes really got me. I fell in love and I didn't know it at the time, but cupid got me real good. Every day during homeroom I got to see her. Best believe I glanced over and marveled at her beauty, but was too scared to do or say much to her. I didn't talk to her until that one day.

In our English class- Ms. McCabe's class- I decided to start sitting next to her, "Man up!" is the only thing I could remember telling myself. I was never in love like this so I guess my anticipation was building. I could no longer hold it in. I knew that at some point I had to make a move, "Hey big earrings...what's your name?" I said with a smirk on my face allowing my toughness to show. "Isabella-Sofia" she said. "And my earrings aren't that big, but you do have a big nose." She quickly said back. "Isabella-Sofia?" I said. "Isn't that like two first names? What was your moms and pops thinking naming you that?" I said looking at her with a confused face. She laughed and mentioned they could not agree on a first name and so they gave her both. I chuckled a bit. "So where you from?"

3

I asked. "The city" she said as if everyone knew which city she was talking about. "What city!?" I exclaimed. "New York City you dummy," she snarled. "Oh, I thought New York was a state not a city." "It is, stupid... all five boroughs make up the city." This was getting real. "Well I'm from Manhattan, we call that the city." She said with a typical New York attitude. Well that makes sense I thought, more confused than I started. I been to NY once and ain't no one told me about no boroughs that make up a city.

But as I was listening to her tell me how her parents moved from New York to Rhode Island a year ago, I could hear the softness of her voice taking me away. I made up my mind that day; one day I would marry Isabella-Sofia.

Chapter 3:

Let Me Get Those Digits!

Getting her number for the first time was like stepping in the name of love. I can't remember if I ever got a girl's number or anything before that. Maybe once, but this one was the most special. The best kind of special. It was during McCabe's English class. That class was my love haven. I loved going to class because I knew I would see my beloved Isabella-Sofia. Her straight unwrinkled hair brought out her cheek bones that flattered you in a kind of way that made you melt. To keep it real, I especially loved when she wore some black panties with her fitted black bra. I mean, I don't know if she bought that lingerie with some Christmas money, but that outfit makes any man's pants get hard. I sure peaked every chance I got. I wasn't trying to be no perv or nothin' just a 9th grader getting some real cinematic views. And best of all, she offered to give me her number! I knew I was ice water cool but to have swag like that meant I was on to something.

We talked about her life and how she wasn't even born in the US. She was born in the Dominican Republic, or DR for short, but let me tell you, she was definitely whitewashed. I mean she pronounced everything correctly. I honestly couldn't believe it. If you're Dominican like I am, you know what I mean. If you're not, well just imagine a Spanish mami speaking perfect English. I mean perfect with no accent. And her vocabulary was off the charts. Big ass words she would use to illustrate a point. I ain't going to lie, soon as I heard a big word come out of her I ran to the library and got me a big ol' vocabulary book to learn me some words! I even carried the book by hand so she could see I wasn't playing around. I was trying my hardest to impress her. I had to be my smartest to have a chance. I probably forgot to tell you she was taking Latin class and was getting all A's on everything. This girl was smart. Really smart. And I had to figure out a way to keep her attention.

Chapter 4:

Sweet Love, Bitter Taste

Back in the day cell phone companies gave you free calling after 9pm. So, that's when the real calling happened. I bet that's the reason they stopped doing away with that... who knows. I knew that I wasn't the best communicator or talker on the phone. I didn't know what to talk about. I mean, like, for real how do you come up with topics off the top of your head? I was getting nervous and thought I would be the worst guy she's ever talked to on the phone. I was going to be that guy! I couldn't let that happen, so I came up with a plan. I'm going to write some topics down and slowly ease my way to anything else we can talk about. My planned worked... well sort of. Once we talked for the first time on the phone, forget the topics. I found out quickly girls love to talk. Her sweet voice was amazing to me. It was like birds chirping, singing their favorite tunes all in unison. I can't remember what we talked about, but I do remember that's when we started to really like each other. In class we grew more and more flirtatious and we even started to *almost* hold hands. I mean I like to think this was the start of it all.

The beginning of a new love. You know the that's-my high-school-sweetheart-girl of my dreams. The one girl you'll never forget about in your life. Every guy has that one girl he'll never forget. Isabella-Sofia was that girl for me. I was totally smitten. I thought about her every day and loved just being around her. For Christmas, I got her a ginger bread man that had an aroma of sweet cinnamon. The scent was really strong and thought it would last a long time. I didn't have really any money to get something nice, but the gingerbread man along with a love poem was all I had to give. I really put my all into that love poem. I was the happiest kid you could imagine. Then one day, the unexpected came. I got the worst news I could ever imagine.

Chapter 5:

If She Only Knew

It was January by this time and her parents let her know they were going back to New York. I couldn't believe it, my heart just dropped. I couldn't believe that the girl I fell in love with was leaving. Like *why* is she leaving is all I could think to myself. That made no sense to me. I was furious inside and could not contain myself. I found out her dad didn't like Rhode Island and figured New York would bring more opportunities. But I didn't care. All I wanted was to have Isabella-Sofia as my girlfriend. Before she left, I remember we had a nice dance at our homecoming event. We danced reggaetón to a song by Don Omar & Daddy Yankee and by then I knew I could not let her love just fade away.

Her final day in little Rhode Island. I will never forget the day, it was **Friday, January 19th, 2007**. It was the day I knew my love would leave and I would have to figure out a way to win back her love. I remember I was sick the day she left and we decided along with her friend to walk to a different bus location than usual. I guess Isabella-Sofia just wanted more time to talk and enjoy our last moments. We took the bus together to her stop, because I was sick that day, she kissed me on the cheek and we gave each other the biggest hug a man can ask for. I wanted deeply to kiss her for the first time, I never got the chance. One day I hoped our lips could touch, but this wasn't this day. As she left, I could feel my heart beat slower and slower for I knew what laid ahead would be a journey that would take perseverance and a desire to be with my one true love.

Chapter 6:

You Got What?

The weekend after she left I never felt so depressed in my life. That whole week, for some reason food didn't taste the same, the sun didn't shine the same, and any other girl I saw just didn't match Isabella-Sofia's beauty. I couldn't help myself and sometimes I would drop a tear a night because I didn't know if this was the end. It was February by this time and we were talking every night even after she left. I learned that she loved music and Greek mythology. She would tell me everything about Greek mythology. Isabella-Sofia knew every story of Greek Gods, she especially loved Aphrodite, the Greek goddess of love. I grew enamored not only by her beauty, but by her wisdom and depth of knowledge. She was very smart in like a liberal, classical kind of way. Just listening to her talk about Greek mythology was like Beethoven playing his famous harmonic notes. I enjoyed every second of our talks on the phone. Then one day, she gave me some news that made me crumble into pieces. She let me know, kind of slyly, that she had a **new boyfriend**. I was heartbroken. It was like I was hit with a ton of bricks and my quest to make her my one and only was now fading away. I could not fathom another man being with Isabella-Sofia. I lived with the guilt but never gave up; I wiped the invisible tears and could only hope I would one day see her again.

Chapter 7:

My Pain Heavy, Her Voice Sweet

By March of that same year, the doctors let me know I had to undergo surgery. To give you background, I was born with a cleft lip, meaning I was born with my lip and nose split open as opposed to closed, like a regular person. I had three surgeries done before I was one year old and even had a special bottle that my mom fed me with. They say ladies love scars, so you could say I used that story to lure the ladies. The surgery involved chipping my hip bone and inserting it in my mouth to straighten my teeth and taking some of my fat from my hip and evening out the split on my lip. Yeah....I know sounds like the craziest thing in the world. I was basically going to be Frankenstein.

I was in crutches, as a small piece of my hip was removed when the surgery was over. I was in serious pain. I couldn't speak from my lip being cut, and my face had dried blood from the surgery. I cleaned it the best I could, but I felt weak. The pain was unbearable. There was always one thing that soothed the pain; talking to Isabella-Sofia.

While she still had her little boyfriend, I stayed in touch. I called less, but still stayed in contact. When I was convalescing from surgery, the only thing that helped the pain was hearing her voice. Just before 9pm, I went to my freezer, grabbed four or five ice cubes, and rolled them up in a napkin to place on my dry bloodied face just so I could comfortably laugh and talk with her on the phone. By the time our conversation was over, the napkin was drenched water dripping all over the phone and floor. It was like every time I talked with her, I could feel the pain easing and my body slowly gaining strength again.

Every time she told her long, deep stories my heart would melt. But while my lips bled from me smiling so much, I didn't care. It didn't matter because I was able to talk to Isabella-Sofia. I felt the true benefits in hearing her voice; a natural healer in itself. Those were some of the few dear moments I remember.

Chapter 8:

The Rotten Apple

May came along that same year and I was now fully back to normal. One day, my mom told me some really great news! She was involved in a network marketing company and there was a major event in New York City. Immediately, the light bulb went on in my head. She let me know she was leaving next weekend and I quickly asked if I could go. This was it! I could finally see Isabella-Sofia for the first time in months. I was so excited I was jumping up and down with joy. In those days, we used AIM to communicate and as I was *aiming* her, I let her know I was going to NY and that we should meet. She was ecstatic about the idea and was making plans to see me. This is was a pinnacle moment in my love journey. It was like a calling from the Greek gods that I could go to New York City; I was on my way to see my queen.

For the ride, I decided to take a book with me. The book was called "Old Man and the Sea" by Ernest Hemingway. It was about an old fisherman in Cuba who, for some eighty days, did not catch a fish. All the fishermen laughed at him because he had not caught fish in months. But one day, in his old wrinkly fishermen outfit and teared up boat, he wandered off to sea for the last time to catch fish and prove to everyone he still had it. In his quest, he ended up catching the biggest marlin he ever laid his eyes on. He tried with all his might to link the heavy marlin on the side of his boat, taking him two days at sea getting the marlin back to base. But on his way back to base, sharks started eating at his marlin. He struggled heavily to get the whole fish back and in the end all he had was the skeleton. The next day, fisherman who laughed at him marveled at the size of the fish he had caught, even though it was just the skeleton, they measured it and marveled at the biggest fish ever caught. The old man never got to claim the marlin, but was respected among his fishermen. I loved the story because the old man never gave up. Some would say he came up short, others would respect his hustle.

When we got to the event in NYC, it was around 10am. I quickly asked my mom for the phone and called Isabella-Sofia. I was so nervous. The moment was turning surreal for me and I was getting anxious to see the girl of my dreams. "Hey Isabella-Sofia! I made it to NY!" She sounded excited but also distant. I asked if she wanted to know my location so we could meet up. But then she told me the worst news I could ever imagine. Her little brothers were sick and she had to take care of them and could not see me. "What?" I was stunned. I had traveled 300 miles to see her and now I could not. I was furious. We talked for ten or so minutes, but after I just couldn't talk anymore. I gave the phone back to my mom and paced around the building for four hours until the event was over. Millions of thoughts running through my mind. When the event was over, we drove back to RI. My mom tried to console me and say that sometimes life gets in the way of things we really want. I had fully put all my emotions towards seeing Isabella-Sofia that day and, well, I fell short. Deep inside I knew I couldn't give up.

Chapter 9:

She Loves Me, She Loves Me Not

By Sophomore year, and every Valentine's day and Christmas I would send Isabella-Sofia a gift or a card. I knew there was nothing I could do but stay in touch and be relevant in her life, even though she was three hundred miles away. She still had the same boyfriend and I could tell I was losing her. We now only talked when we had some free time and kept our conversation light. It was no longer deep conversation like before. We no longer spoke on the phone. Now the new method of communication was texting, AIM, and around that time, Myspace had just come out. I was on her *top 5* and she was on mine, but I wasn't her *top* friend.

Sophomore year, I worked a bit selling DVDs at various flea markets. I then started working at Panera Bread. The coolest thing about working at Panera Bread was that my best friends worked across the street at the local creamery. I never had a ride after working the night shift, which ended at 10pm, so most times I would go visit my best friends at the creamery and stay there, until their shift ended at 12am if I was lucky, but most times 1am to hitch a ride. For those two or three hours, I would ask my best friend Robby for his phone, which at that time was a *Sidekick 2*. We have the iPhone X now. There was a huge difference in how texting and AIM was done. Now there is no AIM, to give you perspective. I would ask for his phone because through AIM I could talk to my beloved Isabella-Sofia. We laughed and enjoyed our conversations. Many nights, I wished that I was there with her in New York, but unfortunately that didn't happen sophomore year.

One day, she told me something I would never forget. Isabella-Sofia told me what love felt like. She said love was like you were floating on clouds, she said it felt like you were in a world filled with joy. Sadly, she wasn't in love with me. She was madly in love with her boyfriend at the time, yeah the same one she connected with when she left Rhode Island. I was heartbroken and hopeful at the same time.

Heartbroken because I wanted to be the first romantic person she fell in love with. I wanted to let her know that I loved her. But, while it wasn't me in this case, something told me to never give up and always go for my girl. I was hopeful because we still messaged each other often and for me, that was enough to stay in the game. Although she wasn't in love with me I needed to see her again. I didn't know how, but I knew that one day I'd be with her even if it was just for one day.

Chapter 10:

Is There a Chance?

Twelfth grade came along and we were still *lightly* talking. It was now senior year and high school would be over soon. All throughout eleventh grade we grew distant. We talked a few times, but she was still madly in love with her boyfriend. I really couldn't explain it, high school was happening and we very busy with our studies. I was still working and playing football and even started the chess team, which was pretty cool at that time. Isabella-Sofia was probably busy getting A's in school and living life. Also, probably still with the boyfriend. I started to message Isabella-Sofia again and slowly, we began talking again. My hair style at the time was curls for the girls and I'd like to say I had some real *swag*. She still had beautiful straight hair that caressed her soft, gentle neck. We would sometimes exchange pictures, nothing too crazy. Myspace gave you access to pictures, too, so I was able to see her pretty often.

Then one day, out of the blue, we decided to set up a day to see each other. I mean really, after two years I'd finally get to see Isabella-Sofia. I was ecstatic to make the trip. I was old enough I could be by myself and, she was old enough to leave the house and hang out with a *friend*. So we set up a Saturday to go and I was off. I took what everyone called in my area the 'Spanish bus' also known as Barahona Transportation. If you didn't know by now I'm Dominican. Well, I was born in the United States but my mom only spoke Spanish. We carried Dominican culture. Anyway, so I took the Dominican Spanish bus from Providence, Rhode Island to the Big Apple. New York City! I couldn't believe it. Here I was chasing the girl of my dreams, the girl I've loved for two years, and I was going to see her again. She probably didn't know I wanted to marry her, but in my mind I was just getting started. I assumed It would take a long time, so I had to start somewhere. You best believe I put on my best outfit. I told my Spanish barber to give me the *sazon caliente* style! That meant I needed the best haircut he could give. If he normally took an hour cutting my hair, I wanted two. I mean everything had to be perfect. I even tipped the guy extra. My 'curls for the girls' hair was on point. I had short thin curls, that gave me a really cool look. I definitely had an aura of confidence going to New York.

The bus ride was really cool. They picked you up at your house and dropped you off anywhere in Manhattan, door to door for like twenty-five bucks.

It was an enjoyable three hour ride with like, eleven other Dominicans and always one random ethnicity that somehow knew of the bus too. This time, I think we had a Greek person, Yassou Tikanis! I mean you put just 3 Dominicans in one van and you'll see what fun looks like, put eleven and you got yourself a real bus ride! Tunes of Bachata music all ride long! Anthony Santos, Raulin Rodriguez, Frank Reyes played until you started dancing on the bus yourself. As we were nearing New York City, I was getting super nervous. Isabella-Sofia lived in the Washington Heights section of New York. It was the mecca for Dominicans coming from the Island to start a new life. Even this day if you go to New York City and head to the Washington Wcights section, you'll see nothing but Spanish commerce stores all over. My palms were getting sweaty as I was approaching the lunch spot we were to meet at. I really didn't have any prep on what to say or do, but what I did do was bring a wad of cash with me. I had worked many years in high school, so by this time I wasn't like *balling* or nothin' but I could now buy a full pie of pizza no more dollar slices. I think I brought with me, like three or four hundred dollars. Fifty had already been set aside for the transportation, so I had a few hundred to spare. I never spent that much in one day, but for a day with Isabella-Sofia I would spend it all. As the driver began to approach the diner I was getting flashbacks of when we first met and how much she meant to me. I couldn't wait to see her again. I was like a kid in a candy store just so excited to see her again. Finally, my day had come!

Chapter 11:

A Portrait Worth a Thousand Words

A s I sat waiting for her in the diner, I quickly popped like four mints in my mouth. I was so ready to meet the person I admired for so many years. There, walking in, was Isabella-Sofia. She still had it! She looked so pretty in her flowery dress. The kind of girl you can bring to your momma any day. She had on these red pearl earrings, and her straight, ironed hair made way for her beautiful smile to crevice in her dazzling beauty. It was the smile that brought me back to when I first met her. And her eyes, those bold poised eyes were so charming. We gave each other the biggest hug maybe for like, five minutes straight. I loved every moment of it. We then sat down and had a little lunch. She got something real light, like a slice of pizza and a soda. I really didn't care what I got. I knew my job was to make her feel special and show her a great time. Of course, as a man I paid for everything. We took the A train to 42nd street and got to see New York City's bright lights. We went to many stores, including the M&M store, the wax celebrities place, and a couple of others that were pretty cool. Then, we walked into this one building that had a bowling alley. The plan was to go bowling together. Bowling was so much fun. I got to teach her a few lessons, but then found out she played on the low, either that or it was my first time bowling, I'll leave that up to you. I think the best part was that we got to laugh and play together. We ordered some light snacks while we talked for a bit, and then we left.

As we were walking down 42nd St., I noticed old Asian men drawing portraits. They had their little benches and were showcasing their art. They were drawing human caricatures and I just thought that was the coolest thing in the world. I immediately took a seat and asked Isabella-Sofia to sit next to me so we could have them draw us. I really didn't know how much it would cost, but I didn't care. They say a picture is worth a thousand words. In my case, worth the greatest love book ever written. The guy still charged me a whopping $70 dollars!! I tried not to flinch too much when the guy said seventy, and naturally growing up broke, I said, "How much!?" "$70" he said in his accent. I said, "oh okay", reaching into my thinning wad of cash. I never paid that much for some sneakers, let alone a picture-so I had to hustle the price a bit. "Can you do sixty?" I said. "No, Seventy", he clapped back. I said, I only got 60. "Ok sixty but no glue," said the man in a scuffled, cut up accent. He sounded like the older men in the movie Mulan; where the men just talk in their dialect. Isabella-Sofia looked at me, and with that look, I gave the guy the $70. I could have fought this price game and got my portrait with no glue to hold the frame, but at that moment I didn't want to look like some cheap guy. I got my portrait with the glue that smelled pretty wild, thanked the guy and gave him a-I just got hustled- look, too. It's not fun getting hustled like that. I'm usually the one hustling people for tips, or to buy an extra DVD, not the other way around. But nonetheless, I got the portrait. It was superb! A cool Spanish kid with curls for the girls and a beautiful mami looking so dazzling in her pretty dress. Right on the corner of the portrait was the date **April 3rd, 2010**. I'll never forget that date, just like I'll never lose that portrait. Every place I've moved I've taken the portrait with me to remind me of Isabella-Sofia.

It was the first time I got to see my queen since she first left Rhode Island. By the end of the day, my bus was coming back to pick me up and we had to head back. It had been a long fun filled day and I was definitely very happy. She was too! You could see the glow in her smile when we were together. She was still with her boyfriend, and she did bring him up once, but only once, so it didn't bother me too much. I really wanted to give her a kiss but just felt it wasn't the right moment. I mean, like, I had waited so long to be with Isabella-Sofia that I knew if I didn't try now I would probably never get the chance again. We gave each other another big hug. Not knowing if I would ever see her again, I leaned in but chickened out at the last minute. We were going away for college soon and sadly, I missed out on the kiss of a lifetime. I promised myself I would get one more chance but it wasn't going to be today.

Chapter 12:

She Won't Say Yes

It was now May of Senior year and prom season was right around the corner. I was class president at my school, so you could say I was a bit popular. I was on the football team and my chess team, which I was captain of, had just won a state championship. But despite all the popularity, I had trouble securing a prom date. I was organizing the prom event, so I was running around and really didn't put time into a getting a date. Of course, the only real person I wanted to go with was Isabella-Sofia, but she was 300 miles away and I thought it was just too much of a stretch to ask someone that far. So I scratched that idea and started to think about other options. I casually liked a few girls and even had a few girlfriends throughout high school, so I thought it would be easy.

The first girl I asked was named Tiffany. She was so sexy, and was the quiet type until she got to know you. So I asked Tiffany out to prom. She said she would let me know in two days since she had to ask her parents for permission. I thought it was a phony excuse that was a nice way to tell me no. I took it as a no, and apparently I was right. After three days waiting, I got no response. She just brushed it aside. Boy, I got swerved! My second prom target was a girl name Lizbeth. Now, Lizbeth was real pretty. A light skinned girl that carried herself in such an elegant way. Her natural beauty sprung out just by her passing you by. I asked her to prom as well and she said that I needed to wait a day. Man, I had horrible luck getting a date for prom and I was class president! I wasn't like the most good looking guy around, but I had some looks. Don't play yourself now your boy Manny had it going on. So I waited the next day, and Lizbeth then told me she had chosen some other guy to take her to prom. There we go again. I was just thinking of not going all together. But I decided to take another chance and ask out another girl named Genesis. Genesis was caramel, like Isabella-Sofia and had a body shaped like model. She was in my AP science class and was fine looking. Yeah, I can definitely go to prom with her, I thought to myself. So one day after class, I pulled Genesis aside and asked if she was going with anyone to prom. At this point, everyone had a date, so if you didn't have one by then, you were left out. She said she didn't have a prom date, so I swooped in like a vulture catching his prey, and asked if she would go to prom with me. She then sighed and said she was not going to senior prom this year. "Really?" I said. She said "yeah I was thinking of just going with my girlfriend and having a good time." Well, that was strike three. I was out. No prom date and I was forced to go because I was class president. I wasn't happy at all and had to live with not having a date to go to my *own* prom. You win some you lose some, I thought.

Chapter 13:

City Dreams

Something magically happened one night after my three rejections, a week before prom. It was like the goddess of love, Aphrodite, had answered my calling. I got a text from Isabella-Sofia. I was wondering how a text came from her at this time around. It was around May time, prom season time, and I knew she had her date all set. She was still with her boyfriend... or so I thought. She let me know they had broken up after three years together. I was shocked and excited at the same time. During our talk, Isabella-Sofia mentioned that she was going to her prom, but didn't have a date, or really that her date bailed on her. I guess her ex-boyfriend and her were having issues. "No need to fear when Manny's here!" I said to myself. She asked me if I would go to prom with her! She asked me! Can you believe it!? After I got that call, I went to my prom even happier that I didn't have a date. I saw all the girls I asked to prom at my prom, Tiffany, Lisbeth, and Genesis but I didn't care, I was going to prom with Isabella-Sofia...in New York City. Ain't nothing was going to stop me from going!

32

Chapter 14:

Every Kiss Begins With 'K'

I was the most excited kid on the block! I never ran naked down the street before yelling like they do on those funny TV commercials, but that day I had that urge to do it. Now, I didn't, but man did jump and down in the shower that night. Manny was going to prom with Isabella-Sofia! I still couldn't believe it. It was a dream come true. Could you believe after four years of chasing the love of my life I finally had the opportunity to go to prom with her. I already had a prom suit and I was still working at that time, so I still had some money left to make a trip to New York. Those trips were a bit expensive, but I didn't care if that meant being with my beloved Isabella-Sofia. I still had to tell my mom I was going to New York to go to a prom. I wasn't entirely sure how she would take the news, whether she would be accepting of the idea. My mom wasn't the strictest parent, but she rarely let me sleep over someone's house, and going to New York City meant sleeping over...coincidentally, my mom was going to Florida for that weekend. I thought to myself, and thought again "What if I just don't tell her?"

"What if I just went to New York City without telling my mom?" That sounded like a really good idea to me. I was not going to take 'No' for an answer and thought this was the best way to do it. So Prom was on Friday night, and luckily for me my mom left Thursday night. Mom, I love you dearly and all, but your boy was going to prom with Isabella-Sofia in New York City!!! To this day, I've never told my mom about my trip to NYC when she left for Florida that weekend. It would be special for me and I was not going to let anything get in the way of it.

I had to plan for prom night with Isabella-Sofia. This time I was going to finally get my long awaited kiss on the lips! None of that cheek stuff, straight lips to lips! But I needed to think of the most romantic way to make my first kiss memorable. I was laying back one day watching TV and a commercial came on that said "Every Kiss begins with K". The light bulb went on in my head! I came up with a plan that I thought would work. The plan was this: I would buy a Hershey's chocolate kiss, put it in a nice small jewelry box like the kind engagement rings go in, and when the moment was right, I'd open it and ask her if she'd like a kiss, smile, then lean in for the real kiss. The plan was amazing and I couldn't wait to do it.

Chapter 15:

My Only Date

Preparation for prom night in New York City was almost, but not quite like when I visited Isabella-Sofia for the first time. Even more perfection was added to the mix. This time, I told my barber he was getting paid double to give me the *best* haircut he's ever given. My fade and cuts had to be pristine. I was not going to take any chances. I bought new shoes for the prom because I remembered my grandma telling me "shoes make the man." I love my grandma and I know she knows a thing or two. I found the best black shiny pair and bought them. Of course, fresh socks and boxers were a must. Look, this was my key moment. Forget everything else, I was living the dream going to prom with Isabella-Sofia.

Talking about prom, my own senior prom went fine. I had good time with my friends, but the real climatic event was my prom in New York City. Isabella-Sofia let me know I would be staying over her house and that I would also meet her family, which included her mom, dad, and two little brothers. "I was staying at her house?" That's what was going on in my mind. I mean, I knew I was going to prom in another state, but I just totally forgot I was staying over. I had to try my hardest to make her parents like me so the *quest* to be Isabella-Sofia's prom date was now becoming a journey. I took the Dominican bus once more, and again 11 Dominicans and 1 odd ethnicity were on there. This time it was a Nigerian women. She was real cool and vibed with us just fine. Also, this time the bus was taking me directly to her house. *Her* House! The bus ride went smooth as pie, and by 8pm I arrived to the front of her house. *Washington Heights Baby*! Where the pastelito and flavored ice cream guys were seen in every corner. I loved the aroma and vibe of this particular section of the city, it reminded me of real culture. Her place was this grey brick building that had like 50 units inside. I was greeted with a big hug at the door and felt welcomed by her parents. I think they appreciated the fact I actually made it. This kid came all the way from Rhode Island, which most people forget is a state, to go to prom with their daughter. Of course they asked a bunch of questions, but once I passed the "he's-a-good-kid-phase", I was in. They treated me well, gave me some food, and also showed me where I would be sleeping; across the room from Isabella-Sofia. In other words, no funny business.

Chapter 16:

The Right Moment

Her father was an honest and hardworking man. I looked him in the eye, man to man, and thanked him for welcoming me into his home.. I also thanked her mother, who resembled Isabella-Sofia, only with lighter skin. Isabella-Sofia was a light caramel color. Her little brothers were cool too! Two little bros just wanting to play videos games; regular teenagers living the life. By now, it was 9-9:30pm, and Isabella-Sofia was making the final touches to her hair and dress. Ok, it was time! Isabella-Sofia had on the most amazing dress I've ever seen. She wore a pearl red colored dress that made even the moon glisten with more vigor. She looked marvelous, her hair was nice and curly dangling behinds her shoulders. You can tell when a girl gets pretty to go somewhere nice, they really know how to do it right. To me, she was prettiest girl on the planet and she was *my* date to prom!

The limousine was waiting for us outside and inside was a group of her friends. They were so eager to meet me and see who Manny was. The first friend I met went by the name of Leona. She was like the coolest person you could ever hang out with. She was Haitian and smart just like Isabella-Sofia. She was her best friend, and to be honest, the sweetest person in the world. Leona was funny and complemented Isabella-Sofia on her outfit. You could tell she was more than just a friend. This was like her ride or die friend; that one friend you can put your total trust on. Everyone should have a friend like Leona in their life. I really liked Leona because she the first person that believed in us. That meant a lot to me that she thought we made a great couple. She could see we really liked each other. As I was getting introduced to her other friends, I nudged my tuxedo pants to make sure I had the jewelry box. I had bought a nice blue suede jewelry box and put the Hershey's Kiss inside the jewelry box just before we left her house. I was going to wait for the perfect moment to present my kiss. I couldn't wait to kiss Isabella-Sofia. I just had to find the right moment.

Chapter 17:

The Melted Chocolate

The event was in some real nice place in downtown Manhattan. This wasn't Washington Heights- this was bright city lights, some way upper middle class area in Manhattan. The place had a real nice balcony overlooking the city. The music playing wasn't bad. Nice and light while we had our dinner. Most people at our table were surprised I had traveled all the way from Rhode Island. Many confused it for Long Island, until I corrected them. Soon enough, the real music came on! That hip-hop-dance-to-the-floor music. We were now in *my* comfort zone. The last time me and Isabella-Sofia danced was back at Homecoming in Rhode Island. Now, we were dancing in New York and we were going be dancing all night long. I was constantly making sure the jewelry box didn't move too much. It was getting hot and sweaty, and we decided to take a breather and sit down. We just chilled a bit and then I suggested we go to the balcony and see the lights. This was it! I was going to find a nice spot and give her our long awaited kiss.

I was getting nervous as we walked to the corner of the balcony. I mean look, this was my first kiss in four years of chasing Isabella-Sofia. Ohhhh baby, I was ready! I grabbed her hand and we star gazed a bit at the city lights. Then, I lightly brushed her hand over to me so we could be face to face, smiling, and I said, " Isabella-Sofia, I got you something!" as I was reaching for my pocket, she said, "Really!?" You could tell she was a bit confused but went along with it anyway. I reached for my pocket and pulled out the jewelry box, her eyes gazing at the small box. I anxiously opened the box, looked at her bold beautiful eyes and asked, "Would you like a kiss?" We both looked at the Hershey's Kiss and something about it looked funny. The Hershey's Kiss had completely melted! I couldn't believe it! We looked at it and we both laughed, I then leaned in slowly, and give her a kiss. Her lips were passionate and sensitive, the kind that make you want to curl your toes and dream of kisses under the moonlight. My first kiss with Isabella-Sofia was the most special moment in my life. We let the romantic vibe of the night take us away.

We were kissing for like thirty seconds, when we heard a calling…"Isabella-Sofia!" someone shouted. Leaning into the corner of the balcony, it was none other than her best friend Leona. She didn't know what we were doing in the corner of the balcony, but once she saw us, she smiled and knew we were just two love birds enjoying our night. "We're about to do group pictures," she said hesitantly as to not stop us, but by then we had stopped kissing. Isabella-Sofia blushingly looked at me and was off with her friends to take pictures. As she left, I dozed off looking at the New York City lights. What a magical and memorable night. The night I finally kissed Isabella-Sofia.

Chapter 18:

A Little Envy Makes Honey

By the end of senior year, we were both off to college and I knew there would be *sometime* between us until the next time we saw each other. I ended up going to Bentley University, a renowned business school in Massachusetts close to Boston and Isabella-Sofia attended the prestigious Fordham University in the Bronx. My first semester at school, I did what any young handsome guy would do: chase girls and live a life full of freedom. I messed with some girls here and there and even fell slightly for this one girl. Her name was Amanda. But every time I would sleep over Amanda's dorm, I would always sneak on the computer when she fell asleep to talk to Isabella-Sofia via Facebook. Yeah, by now Facebook was the main form of communication, and of course texting too. No more AIM, those days I still remember like it was yesterday. When Amanda fell asleep, we would exchange messages for hours, and if Amanda asked what I was doing I would always just say I was working on some paper, or messaging a buddy of mine. She knew I was up to something, but never asked. All I knew was that if I was going to do anything, I would stay in touch with the love of my life. I told Isabella-Sofia about Amanda, that I had been seeing her a few times here and there. I could tell she was getting a bit jealous of the whole ordeal and I noticed she would always ask how it was going with Amanda. "Do you really like her? How did you guys meet? You guys hang out a lot?" I guess me hanging out with Amanda strengthened our attraction. It was getting sweeter and sweeter to know that Isabella-Sofia was starting to like me on a deeper level. I was feeling real happy inside, and in the midst of it all, a few thoughts ran through my mind: I needed to be with Isabella-Sofia, I didn't have an idea of how to do it, but I knew I needed to come up with a plan.

Winter vacation came and I was back in Rhode Island working at Panera Bread. I managed to get my job back for the month of December and half of January. It gave me some much needed funds to help me pay for books. During that vacation, Isabella-Sofia visited me in Rhode Island. I thought that was nice of her to come for the day, almost like when I visited her, senior year. The day she visited me, we had no heat. I remember they had cut off the heat two days before and I had slept on the couch in the living room, wrapped up in the thickest blankets you could find. She was at my door by the time I got ready, and we off to start our day.

Chapter 19:

Such a Sure Thang

She looked so beautiful. It was snowing by this time and I could feel how cold she was just giving her a hug. Her face, while cold, held this warmth that just assured me everything would be alright. I was embarrassed a bit because I was sleeping in the living room and you could tell something was off. I took a shower and got dressed quickly to take advantage of the day with Isabella-Sofia. Deep inside, I was so happy and loving the fact that we were hanging out together. I decided to give her a tour of her old house and places she used to visit when she lived in Rhode Island. We kissed a few times in my car. My car at the time was a '92 Toyota Corolla with 250k miles on it. It was real love. Just us two making out in my *hoopty*. She was my Bonnie and I was her Clyde.

We went ice skating downtown. Funny how your masculinity goes out the window when you attempt to ice skate and fall so many times. There's no other way to deal with it than to laugh. We had fun together ice skating. I pushed her a few times to see what would happen, and well, she didn't fall down unless someone came down with her. Guess who that someone was? Ice skating with my queen was an experience, a true way of enjoying each other's presence. We went to Starbucks afterwards, and enjoyed some hot coffee. Well, she did, at least. I was going along with the idea that men don't need anything to keep them warm. That was stupid of me. I sat there warming up naturally while she sat there so warm with her cup of coffee. But, I didn't mind. I was with Isabella-Sofia having a great time. By afternoon, the bus came to pick her up. I gave her a final kiss goodbye and thought of ways to express our affection even further.

Chapter 20:

Love In You

It was now sophomore year in college, and I was living in a four bedroom dorm with the wildest guys on campus. We threw parties like you couldn't believe. But in the midst of it all, Isabella-Sofia texted me one day and asked if she could visit me at Bentley. What? Visit me at school for the *weekend? Oh yes baby girl, you can visit any time you want!* My mind at this moment was going crazy. Prior to her visit we had sexted but I didn't know how far it would go. Like one night, I asked her a few questions about different positions and what her thoughts were, to my surprise she gave me some responses that definitely got me aroused.

A week before her scheduled visit, I looked up every way to increase my foreplay game, and every way to make our night the most special. I had friends of mine that were girls that prepped me a bit, and one even offered to clean my room. That was real nice of them, they knew that I was excited to see baby girl. I even ran laps for that week getting my body in shape, and raising my stamina levels to make sure I was good. You could say I was going nuts. I told my roommate at the time that I would be using the room for the weekend. He figured going home for the weekend was best; I mean I was talking about Isabella-Sofia the whole week. My brother from another mother, Aaron, was a real friend that really looked out that day. I had the room to myself for the whole weekend.

She arrived at Bentley on that Friday night. Of course, we had something to eat after her long four hour journey from New York. The minute we went back to my place, sparks started to fly. Once we got to my room, I grabbed her soft hands and looked her in the eyes. It was those bold poised eyes that gave me the courage to go after my baby girl, I leaned in and her kissed her like it was our first time. Flashbacks of when she left on the bus her last day in Rhode Island came to my mind; I gave her the most passionate kiss my lips could muster. After caressing her a bit, she went to her luggage bag and asked If I'd ever used a glow in the dark condom. This is just what I loved; some artistic vibes on a sexual level. Trying to stay cool as water, I said, "Not a glow in the dark, but flavored yes." I gave the best poker face I could, knowing I was lying. We kissed until our hearts melted unto our warm bodies. To set the mood just right, I learned that foreplay is a man's best friend. As we dimmed the lights, we slowly become one. All night, we indulged in our sexual love. When we finally went to sleep, I looked up and thought of Aphrodite, the goddess of love. She had blessed two special people that night. Our night was magical; one to always remember.

Chapter 21:

All I Need In This Life, Is Me and My Girlfriend

After Isabella-Sofia left for that weekend, all I could think of was the Tupac song, "Me and My Girlfriend." I wanted Isabella-Sofia to be my girlfriend. I really didn't have a plan but I knew I had to make her mine. That summer after Sophomore year, I was able to land an internship with one of the biggest Pharmaceutical companies in the world, Johnson & Johnson. I was a financial analyst and was making $20 dollars an hour. It was the most money I've ever made at a job. Before that, I was scrubbing the floors at Panera Bread. I thought I made it! I grew up broke with visions of making it big one day, and so this was definitely the right step. Then one night, the light bulb in my head went on. What if I decide to use some of the money I made and go to New York every weekend? As much as I could, at least? That way, I could see my beautiful Isabella-Sofia. That way, I could see her every weekend. I began to think of the possibilities.

One night, I finally made my decision; I would go to New York and ask Isabella-Sofia to be my girlfriend. I had looked up stories of couples in long distance relationships, talked with a friend of mine named Rafael, who was also in a long distance relationship, and did anything I could to see what how couples stay in love. I didn't care about the drawbacks; I was going to make Isabella-Sofia my girlfriend and I was going to do it next weekend.

The weekend came and I met Isabella-Sofia at Fordham University. She was living in the dorms for the summer and she had a little get-together that day. I got to meet some of her other friends, and even Leona was there! We clicked right away, like good friends who haven't seen each other in a while. She was really advocating for us to be together- Leona was the best. That night we laughed, had a good time, smoked and drank, like college students having a fun time. Just when everyone left by 4am, Leona confided in me and told me Isabella-Sofia had a massive crush on me. Once she left, and we had some alone time, I grabbed Isabella-Sofia's hand, half drunk and said, "Isabella-Sofia, I can't even front, you make me the happiest guy on Earth, would you be my girlfriend?" We both laughed because that was a really corny line to say. She kissed me with her soft warm succulent lips and said, "tomorrow I will let you know". That night, Aphrodite gave me another night to remember.

Morning came, she stared into my eyes and said, "You know what you said last night? Did you mean it?" I thought about the almost six years I had spent chasing Isabella-Sofia's love and how her voice always warmed my heart. I said, "Of course, you're everything I ever wanted." After those words left my lips, she kissed me again and said, "Boy, you make my mind go crazy. I would love to be your girlfriend." The date was **June 8, 2012**. I will never forget the day Isabella-Sofia became my girlfriend.

Chapter 22:

Reaching Close for Love

That summer, I started traveling to New York City more often, since Isabella-Sofia was now my girlfriend. I knew I had to come up with a plan to be with her full-time. I wanted to see Isabella-Sofia every day, and I had to come up with something good. By then, I was traveling from Providence to New York every other weekend, and soon I was going to college again for junior year and the commute would be longer; from Boston to New York. I was involved in a business group at my school, and we had a major networking conference coming up in Las Vegas. At the conference, you could secure internships for the following summer. The light bulb went on again. What if I tried my best to get an internship in New York?" That would change everything. So that was it! That was my mission: Secure an internship in New York City so I can be with my beloved Isabella-Sofia.

At the conference, there were hundreds of companies. Finance, technology, accounting, management, all kinds of industries. My mind was clear, if the internship was not in New York, I didn't want to know about it. At one table, I saw a few executives sitting, and I decided to introduce myself. They said they were from a private equity firm that had offices in New York and Providence. I was amazed! I quickly got their information and set up an interview. Not so fast, though. They wanted me to go to their executive breakfast to screen me. Other prospecting students wanted internships at the same firm. I had competition, but was one step closer to completing my mission of being in New York.

I was determined. I was not going to lose. No one was going to stop me from securing an internship in New York. I needed to be with Isabella-Sofia. At the breakfast, students tried their best to keep the executive's attention. I employed every chess verbal tactic I could think of. I was former state chess champion, so I used every warfare move I had. I played my best role, and secured an interview for the next day. The interview went amazingly, and in a few hours, I got the call! I got the internship! There was one condition, though. The only position available was in Providence. Shit! They needed an answer at that moment, since they were filling up their spots. I thought about it for a second. I thought about the amazing opportunity, and said, "I appreciate your offer so much, but I cannot accept." I was upset because it was literally in my hometown, and really good money. I found some random guy and asked him if he wanted to get lunch. I had to clear my mind and talk with someone. I felt like I lost the battle. The guy was extremely happy someone actually invited him for lunch. He was complaining most people just take, take and never give.

We talked and then he mentioned he was a recruiter for BNY Mellon. That's a funny name I thought, who would name a company after a fruit? "What does your company do? I said casually. "Asset servicing and custody trading for high net worth clients" He said laughing because I guess he liked our vibe. To me, he didn't seem like a recruiter. He was just some guy I was getting lunch with because I had bad day. Hmmm, thought. That's cool, asset servicing for rich people. He took a real liking in me after we talked about cars, and then asked me what my plans were. I said I was looking for an internship in NYC, in finance. He looked at me with the most stunned face. "You're perfect for the role I have, you're in if you want it, we have like two more spots open!" BNY stands for Bank of New York. It's located on Wall Street! I looked him in the eye and thanked him for the opportunity, and with the biggest smile, said I would love to work for BNY Mellon. I got the internship in New York City on Wallstreet. Battle scars and all, I did it! Next summer I was going to be with baby girl, Isabella-Sofia!

Chapter 23:

A Christmas Season

It was Christmas time and Isabella-Sofia was coming over to visit me again! We were going to exchange our Christmas gifts. I was never big on Christmas gifts, because as a kid I used to get in line when community organizers held Christmas fundraisers, to get gifts. We never had much money, so if I wanted a decent gift I had to hustle my way into getting a gift none of the kids on the line saw. I wanted this Christmas to be different. I made the decision in my mind that I would make this the best Christmas I've ever had.

Isabella-Sofia was going to study abroad the semester after the holidays, and it would not be until May that she would be back in the States. It was another road I needed to cross, but for Isabella-Sofia I would do anything. For Christmas, she got me a watch and I got her a couple of things: her favorite perfume which was Flower Bomb from Sephora. I learned how to buy at that store. Let me tell you, it's an experience going in there. And if you're a single guy, you're definitely in the right spot! The next thing I got her was a matching shirt that read, "I love TOFU", TOFU meaning Together One. If not F U. I can't remember exactly, but something along those lines. Lastly, the most special gift I got her, made us cry together. I remembered back during one of our visits, she told me about her favorite Latin poem. I wrote it down in case I found a perfect moment to use it. The gift I got her was a calendar that had pictures of us for each month. January, the month she left from Rhode Island to New York, had the last picture we took in Ms. Georges Homeroom Class. After we both laughed and kissed at some of the pictures, I told her to look at the last page; there she saw her favorite Latin poem, <u>Kisses for Catullus</u>:

Let us live, my Lesbia, and let us love,
and let us judge all the rumors of the old men
to be worth just one penny!
The suns are able to fall and rise:
When that brief light has fallen for us,
we must sleep a never ending night.
Give me a thousand kisses, then another hundred,
then another thousand, then a second hundred,
then yet another thousand more, then another hundred.
Then, when we have made many thousands,
we will mix them all up so that we don't know,
and so that no one can be jealous of us when he finds out

how many kisses we have shared.

She was stunned. She kissed me like never before and we both we in complete emotional state; it was a moment I'll never forget. Our lips kissed a thousand times- only to keep it a secret so the world would not know how much love we shared. Till this day, that's my favorite Christmas.

Chapter 24:

Three Words For Me

It was now January 2nd of the new year, 2013. In two days, Isabella-Sofia was leaving to study abroad in the Dominican Republic. I thought her going to DR was cheating to go study abroad since she was Dominican, if you ask me, but I had family there so it was easy for me to plan to visit. I went to visit her in NYC, and like always, I would have to sleep in an opposite room. One midafternoon her parents were not home and we had the apartment to ourselves. Aphrodite once again let us loose and wild. It was a fun time, to say the least. When we ended our escapade on her mother's living room couch, she said something no girl has ever told me.

She whispered in my ear the three words that made it all worth it: *I love you*. I was shocked; completely love struck. That moment, flashbacks raced through my mind; the long distance, the years I spent chasing her love, and the persistence I kept to have my baby girl close to me were all worth it to hear her say those words. The man code I was taught was wait one week to say it back. I tried to keep my integrity and held for a moment. "You really mean that?" I said. She looked at me with her soft smile and said, "Yes baby, I do" and nodded her head as to show me that it was real. Her love for me was real. I sat back, looked in her eyes and let her know that my one true love was right in front of me. "I loved you since the first time I met you." I said. She left for DR the next day. It would be a few more months until I would see my love, Isabella-Sofia.

Chapter 25:

My Valentines

I could not live with not seeing baby girl for five months after we had just recently become a couple. Just before I left in March, for Valentine's Day, I had to be super creative in expressing my love. I was able to reach a friend of Isabella-Sofia via Facebook named Gabriela that was studying abroad with her. She was one of the few friends Isabella-Sofia really connected with, and I reached out to see if she could help me plan an amazing Valentine's day for my sweetheart. I asked her best friend if she could pretend to buy a valentine's day for her mother, and to say she needed Isabella-Sofia's help to pick it out. Unknowingly, Isabella-Sofia picked out a really nice one, and I had her friend purchase the card. I sent some money and a little extra so that all costs could be covered. I knew Isabella-Sofia's favorite chocolates were Ferrero Rocher. I begged Gabriela to find them in DR. Anything for my baby girl. Valentine's Day came, and I had a few gifts that were coming. Right at 8am, someone knocked on Isabella-Sofia's door. First, a delivery of Ferrero Roche chocolates, ten minutes later the card she chose with

Gabriela, and twenty minutes after that, her final gift; a chocolate covered Rose. Happy Valentine's Day, Sweetheart!

Chapter 26:

That Statue Has Breasts?

Location: *Santiago, Dominican Republic*

During March break of my Junior year, I booked a trip to visit Isabella-Sofia in the Dominican Republic. It was going to be my birthday week and I wanted nothing other than to be with Isabella-Sofia for my special day. I had some family in DR, so when I arrived I was able to show Isabella-Sofia my family. They all liked her and found her to be unique. Just before Isabella-Sofia left abroad she had changed her hairstyle from straight, to now Afro puffy like the style in the 80's. I thought it was the dopest hairstyle ever.

In the Dominican Republic we visited place like the *Monumento* in Santiago. It is the biggest structure in the second largest city on the Island. The top of the structure had a big fat lady with her bosom out. Legend says Trujillo, the dictator who ruled sixty years ago, had built a large pointy cathedral that symbolized his sexual prowess and the women with her breast out to showcase his dominance of masculinity. That guy was crazy, but I have to admit he was creative.

We spent my birthday at a lounge called Dubai with her friends, but when the night was over Aphrodite was once again able to help a Spanish brother out and provide me with the best hotel that was available. Then came our trip. I planned a trip to a nice resort where we went zip lining, horseback riding, and even jumped off 14 waterfalls they called *Los 27 Charcos de Aqua*. My trip to visit Isabella-Sofia was full of adventures and fun; I couldn't wait to be with her in New York. It was only three months away.

Chapter 27:

Love & Hustle
In New York City

Part 1

The end of May came along and I was making my way for New York City. I had an internship on Wall Street which gave me enough money to live on my own, and I had a girlfriend I loved and wanted to be with. My first day in New York was one to never forget. My cousin let me stay in his apartment in the Bronx for two days; it was a stretch to find an apartment in that time frame, but I was determined. I entered the Bodega in front of the projects by the Marbill Hill Section in the Bronx, and right away saw some action. "Imma get all my peoples and we going light this shit up! Give me the damn change! I live right in front and we ready" an agitated customer said. I was in the middle of the warfare and quickly paid for my water and left. I grew up in the inner city and it wasn't the safest all the time, but New York was a different animal.

"Go to Broadway in Manhattan by 168th" my cousin instructed. "Tell 'em you looking for a room to rent and hustle what you came for P." He loved Mobb Deep and always used the 'P' in Prodigy as a reference to name you. As I walked to the realty place on Broadway, some stylish, well-groomed Spanish lady said, "Ok honey, *mira*- look is $150 dollars upfront to get a list of rooms available in Manhattan- then you go to the places and see if the owner likes you." This should be interesting, I said to myself. I got my list, but I knew exactly where I wanted to live. *Washington Heights, Baby*! Where my beautiful lived. See, I wanted to be as close as I could to Isabella-Sofia. Our love for each other was stronger than ever and I was committed to doing my best to living as close as I could to her. The first apartment I went to was in the Bronx on the Grand Concourse. As soon as I walked in the place, I saw a guy smoking something funny in the corner and another guy with a busted nose. The room was okay and could work, but something wasn't right. Forget everything else, it was too far from Isabella-Sofia.

After going to five different places, I landed one that was just two blocks from Isabella-Sofia's house. I did not care about the condition. The owner, an old lady in her 80's, wanted $150 a week with no kitchen access. I had to hustle that the best way I could. I gave her the story that everyone likes to hear; The American dream story. I told her how I grew up broke and told her now I had an internship on Wall Street, showed her my commitment letter from BNY Mellon, and let her know I could pay her every Friday morning. I got the price down to $125 and got live next to a smoking hot girl who lived just two blocks away! My beautiful Isabella-Sofia.

Part 2

I lived right next to Isabella-Sofia and we were living the life we always wanted to live. I would go to my Wall Street job in the morning and by late afternoon I would always hang out with Isabella-Sofia. We loved holding hands, strolling through Central Park and Belvedere Castle. When we walked by, you could hear the birds chirping for our love, mesmerized by our affection for each other. Isabella-Sofia introduced me to all her friends and family as her boyfriend. That was just an amazing feeling. At that moment, I felt true love; being with Isabella-Sofia felt like I was floating on clouds, like I was in a world filled with joy. I was the happiest man on Earth.

Part 3

We were finally together and life was good. I would often go to Isabella-Sofia's house and talk with her mother and father. They were great people and liked me as her boyfriend. They knew how hard I worked to make this happen and so they always welcomed me with open arms. One day in Isabella-Sofia's room, I noticed something reminiscent of when we first met. In her drawer, she had all the love letters, Christmas and Valentine's day cards I had ever given her. I couldn't believe it! Even the gingerbread man was there and it still smelled like sweet cinnamon! I was amazed the smell was still there after so many years. Isabella-Sofia then pulled out an old notebook and confessed to me something that made melt to a thousand pieces of happiness.

Part 4

The notebook had a piece about me. This was the notebook she wrote in that chronicled her life since High School. It was where all her thoughts were written. She let me know me know that the reason why her and ex-boyfriend broke up was because of what was inside. In it she wrote, "The only person I wanted to make love with first was Manny." I stood, love-shocked and confident I was with my one true love. I also had a confession to make: She was the first person I ever had sex with.

Part 5

I spent three and half months in New York and now it was time to leave and finish my senior year of college. I had enjoyed a summer with the most beautiful girl in the world. I was determined to marry Isabella-Sofia one day. After we kissed for the last time in New York, on the bus ride back home I came up with my plan on how to one day marry Isabella-Sofia. I knew she loved Greek Mythology, and so my plan would be to take her to Greece and after sightseeing all the beautiful Greek temples, propose to her in front of Aphrodite, the Greek goddess of love. She had guided us all these years to finally be together. Thereafter, we would hold our ceremony in the beaches of Dominican Republic. I couldn't wait to make it happen. But of course, the story didn't end that way.

Chapter 28:

Senior Year Slipped

Senior year of college was extremely hectic. We were both in pursuit of any job we could take to make sure we could stay together, but at the same time our love began to slowly fade away. We talked as much we could, but with our post-grad future being the main focus, we barely connected. We talked less on the phone and our conversations we no longer going as smooth. The pressure of it all got to us and we would go a few days without talking. I was heartbroken on the low because I could no longer foresee a plan to be close to Isabella-Sofia. Close to the end of Senior year, I got a message from Isabella-Sofia that made me lose hope. She wanted to know if we should continue our relationship since we just didn't know what would happen next. I confidently said we could try to make plans to live together. It would all be good. I let her know, "Baby, trust me I'll figure it out."

Chapter 29:

Is Love lost?

After college ended, I was able to find a job working in Downtown Boston. I tried my hardest to secure a job in New York, but no offers came in. I received an offer from a bank and was able to land a good job. Isabella-Sofia decided to take some time off after graduation before finding a job. Life after graduation was still very hectic because, it is mainly a point in your life you don't really know how to navigate. After being in school for so long, you really don't know what's next. Isabella-Sofia was able to visit me for that summer after college ended, in May, and we enjoyed a trip together. But something was missing, I couldn't tell if love was being lost or if we just weren't connecting like we once did. I loved my baby girl to the moon and back, but I could just feel the love slipping away.

Chapter 30:

How long Is Love Worth Holding?

I visited Isabella-Sofia by October of 2014. It was still the year we graduated college and I still loved my baby girl. I went with an open mind to visit her knowing it could be my last visit. When we first saw each other, I hugged her as if it was the first time I had seen her back senior year of high school. She still had a slim waist and smooth caramel-colored skin that glistened in the sun. She was beautiful, it was the same girl I fell in love with the first day we met in Ms. George's class.

We ended going out to dinner, but the vibe just wasn't the same anymore. Although we kissed, our kisses no longer held passion. They were basic in their simplest form. I brought up topics of what we could do in the future, and the exchange of ideas were not the same anymore. I knew she was going through some post-college stress, but I would never think it would get in the way of our loving relationship. I could not understand what the problem was.

We visited one of her friends in Washington Heights. The topic of what I would do next in my life, came up. I mentioned I found a job in Boston, but that I was open to moving to New York and mentioned Isabella-Sofia could help me as I transition. Isabella-Sofia looked at me with a shy sudden voice and said, "I don't think I'll be able to help out, you would be on your own." I know she meant that I would do the journey all over but this time I felt I was not getting the support I needed. I was wishing for Isabella-Sofia to comment that we would able to tackle New York together and that we always figure it out. I always tried my best to make our love work. My love and smile had faded a bit when I looked at Isabella-Sofia. I couldn't believe that after all these years our love was coming to an end. When we left, Isabella-Sofia let me know she was going to a school program for the next couple of weekends, and that it would difficult to coordinate seeing each other until after the program was finished. She had told me about the program before, but not that it was only on weekends. The morale was down, the love was lost, and my belief in our companionship was fading away. When we arrived at her house, I grabbed her hand and looked in her eyes, and said, "Isabella-Sofia, I love you but I don't think we can be together anymore and I think we should take a break."

We both went silent, but knew that although we loved each other, things were just not working out anymore. I looked into her deep poised eyes not knowing if it would be the last time we would see each other. I thought about when I was in surgery and her voice was the only thing that helped ease my pain, I thought about the first day she let me know what love felt like, I thought about my deep love for doing anything I could do to live next to her in NYC, and I thought about how this could now be coming to an end.

Chapter 31:

A Love Farewell

A few weeks after we broke up, Isabella-Sofia and I talked once on the phone. We talked about us and how things were going and our families were doing. She brought back some good memories of our times together and even said she would visit me in Rhode Island. It had been a really long time since I heard her say she loved me and I didn't know if she still did. I was anxious to see her again. I couldn't wait to see my love again. The excitement in my heart had me ready for a new chapter with Isabella-Sofia. A love adventure that would last forever. I waited for her to come...I waited, and waited but she never came.

A year and half later, I traveled to New York and met with Isabella-Sofia. When we saw each other, it was a cold hug, no warm anymore like it always was. We hung out for about twenty minutes, and I asked her about her life and how things were going. She exchanged conversation in a pleasant way and then I asked if she had any romantic partners she was involved with. She mentioned she was lightly talking with someone, which meant to me she was single. While she was talking to me, her voice brought me back to Ms. George's class. When I first fell in love. Her bold poised eyes giving me the best memories I could ever imagine. My intuition told me I had maybe one more chance to regain her love. Gently, I looked at her and I slowly grabbed her hand like I always did. I looked into the same eyes that guided me all these years to never give up. I leaned in for a kiss and her final words came out, "*Please don't...* is this what you brought me here for? I'll leave right now if I have to." Those were the last words I remember. I had been completely rejected. I felt so defeated, as if pin needles had pierced through my heart. I completely lost her love. At that moment, I thought about the "Old Man and the Sea." Like the old man, I had persevered through life's biggest challenges to reach Isabella-Sofia's love. With all my might, I did everything I could to make our relationship work. At the end of the journey all the old man had was the skeleton of the biggest marlin anyone had ever caught. All I had was the greatest love story I'll never forget. My dream is still to marry Isabella-Sofia one day and be together until we are old and grey and can't walk anymore. If I had the chance, I would hold her hand until together, we perished away. That was the last time I saw Isabella-Sofia. I will never forget her beautiful smile.

The glue still holds even after all this time.

April 3, 2010

NYC

Always Believe in Love

-Manny Ventura

www.ingramcontent.com/pod-product-compliance
Lightning Source LLC
Chambersburg PA
CBHW020759130626
46554CB00006B/2261